Pigs Have Piglets

by Lynn M. Stone

Animals and Their Young

Content Adviser: Terrence E. Young Jr., M.Ed., M.L.S.
Jefferson Parish (La.) Public Schools

Reading Adviser: Dr. Linda D. Labbo,
Department of Reading Education, College of Education,
The University of Georgia

COMPASS POINT BOOKS

Minneapolis, Minnesota

Compass Point Books
3722 West 50th Street, #115
Minneapolis, MN 55410

For more information about Compass Point Books, e-mail your request to:
custserv@compasspointbooks.com

Photographs ©: Lynn M. Stone

Editors: E. Russell Primm and Emily J. Dolbear
Photo Researcher: Svetlana Zhurkina
Photo Selector: Linda S. Koutris
Design: Bradfordesign, Inc.

Library of Congress Cataloging-in-Publication Data

Stone, Lynn M.
  Pigs have piglets / by Lynn Stone.
      p. cm. — (Animals and their young)
  Includes bibliographical references and index.
  Summary: An introduction to the life cycle of pigs from birth to adult, discussing appearance, food, instinct, and nurturing.
    ISBN 0-7565-0003-6 (lib. bdg.)
    1. Piglets—Juvenile literature. [1. Pigs. 2. Animals—Infancy.] I. Title. II. Series: Stone, Lynn M. Animals and their young.
SF395.5 .S763 2000
636.4'07—dc21   00-008833

Table of Contents

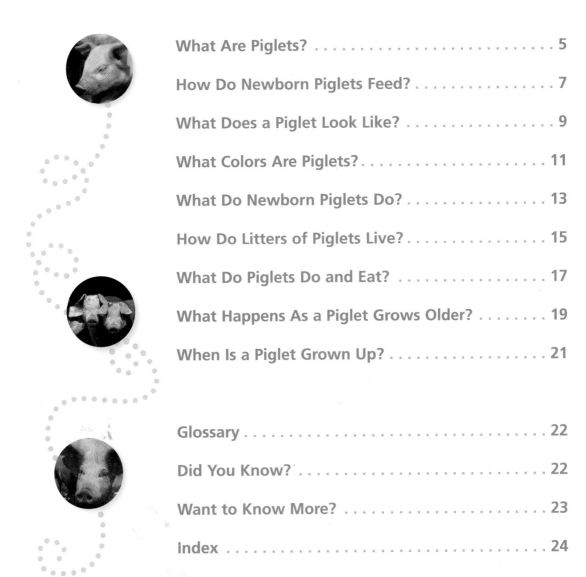

What Are Piglets?

Piglets are the babies of a mother pig, or **sow**. The father pig is called a **boar**. The sow carries her babies inside her body for almost four months.

Then she gives birth to six to twelve piglets. Some kinds, or breeds, of pigs have fewer babies. Some sows have up to twenty-seven piglets! A group of piglets born at one time is called a **litter**.

◄ Piglets are born in litters.

How Do Newborn Piglets Feed?

A piglet gets milk from its mother right after birth. This is called **nursing**. The piglets drink nothing but mother's milk for three weeks.

◄ A litter of colorful piglets drink from their mother.

What Does a Piglet Look Like?

Piglets look like tiny pigs. A newborn piglet weighs about 2½ pounds (1 kilogram). The mother pig weighs about 450 pounds (204 kilograms). The mother pig must be careful not to crush the piglets.

Piglets have long bodies and short, thick necks. Piglets also have a boxy **snout**, or nose, and a curly tail.

Also like their mothers, piglets are covered with long, stiff hairs called **bristles**. But the piglets' bristles are shorter and softer.

◀ Piglets have stubby legs and floppy ears.

What Colors Are Piglets?

Piglets may be a different color from their mother and father. And all the piglets in a litter may not be the same color. That's because the sow and boar are probably different breeds. Most pig farmers in North America raise piglets from parents of different breeds. The piglets may look like one parent or both parents.

◀ Pigs come in many colors!

What Do Newborn Piglets Do?

The youngest piglets spend most of their time, nursing, sleeping, grunting, and squealing. However, little pigs grow quickly and soon become more active.

At five weeks old, piglets weigh 18 to 20 pounds (8 to 9 kilograms). At this age, piglets raised in a barn are separated from their mothers. Then they are **weaned**. Weaned animals eat solid foods and no longer drink their mother's milk.

◄ Piglets grow quickly.

How Do Litters of Piglets Live?

Some pig litters are raised in a pen inside a large barn. Each sow and her litter have a separate pen. Other sows and their litters live in huts.

Litters of piglets don't always get along as they grow older and bigger. They sometimes chase and bite one another.

Pig farmers usually remove the piglets' sharpest teeth at birth. Many farmers also cut the piglets' tails. That stops piglets from biting each other's tails!

◀ Piglets live together in a pen.

What Do Piglets Do and Eat?

Piglets follow their mothers around. They use their snouts like little shovels. Sometimes they find food in the soft soil. They like to eat grubs, corn kernels, or roots. However, they still drink milk most of the time until they are weaned.

Sows living on grassy fields keep a close eye on their litters. If a sow senses danger, she grunts loudly. Her piglets run to her. When she runs to safety, her piglets trot along with her.

◀ There are many things for
piglets to eat on a farm.

What Happens As a Piglet Grows Older?

A pig farmer wants piglets to grow quickly. The piglets grow faster on solid food than on milk. Without the sow's milk, the piglets eat more solid food.

At first, the piglets eat a dry, crusty food called pellets. Two weeks later, the farmer gives them corn and soybean meal. By now the piglets weigh about 20 pounds (9 kilograms). Most adult pigs still eat corn and soybean meal.

Solid food makes pigs grow faster.

When Is a Piglet Grown Up?

At six months old, a young pig weighs about 250 pounds (114 kilograms). Most pigs are shipped to market at this time.

Pigs that are not shipped to market keep on growing. Some pigs live to be fifteen years old. They can weigh more than 1,000 pounds (455 kilograms)—more than a small cow!

Pigs don't wait long to have piglets. Sows are ready to have their first litter when they are six months to eight months old.

It is not long before young pigs have their own litter of piglets.

Glossary

boar—an adult male pig; a father pig

bristles—long, stiff hairs

litter—a group of animals born to the same mother at one time

nursing—drinking milk produced by the mother

snout—the nose of a pig

sow—an adult female pig; a mother pig

weaned—taken away from mother's milk and given solid food

Did You Know?

- Christopher Columbus brought pigs to the Americas.
- There are about 825 million pigs in the world.
- Pigs do not sweat.

Want to Know More?

At the Library

Gibbons, Gail. *Pigs*. New York: Holiday House, 1999.

Royston, Angela. *Pig*. New York: Warwick Press, 1990.

Wolfman, Judy. *Life on a Pig Farm*. Minneapolis: Carolrhoda Books, 1998.

On the Web

Breeds of Livestock: Swine

http://www.ansi.okstate.edu/breeds/swine/

For information about all breeds of pigs

Nature: The Joy of Pigs

http://www.pbs.org/wnet/nature/pigs/

For information about how to keep pigs as pets

Through the Mail

National Pork Producers Council

P.O. Box 10383

Des Moines, IA 50306

For information about the pork industry

On the Road

A big weekend festival is held every September, in Kewanee, Illinois, the official Hog Capital of the World.

Index

About the Author

Lynn M. Stone has written hundreds of children's books and many articles on natural history for various magazines. He has photographed wildlife and domestic animals on all seven continents for such magazines as *National Geographic, Time, Ranger Rick, Natural History, Field and Stream*, and *Audubon*.

Lynn Stone earned a bachelor's degree at Aurora University in Illinois and a master's degree at Northern Illinois University. He taught in the West Aurora schools for several years before becoming a writer-photographer full-time. He lives with his wife and daughter in Batavia, Illinois.